DEUX

DEUX

A 50 X 50 MICRO NOVELLA

RAN WALKER

CONTENTS

For Elle

PREFACE

CREATING THE 50 X 50 MICRO NOVELLA

In 2020, I decided to conduct an experiment. After writing hundreds of 100-word stories, I decided to attempt a novel written entirely in one hundred chapters of one hundred words each. I called it the "100 x 100 Micro Novel" (although I also call it a "Novel in 100-Word Stories"). The fruit of that labor became the book *A Burst of Gray*, with several other books to follow.

Simultaneously, I wondered what a novella would look like if it were composed of fifty chapters of exactly fifty words each (you can see where I'm going with this). This would be a 50 x 50 Micro Novella. I didn't write it immediately, though. I was still compiling collections of 50-word stories (to date, I have two of them, *The Strange Museum* and *Spaceships Don't Come Equipped With Rearview Mirrors*). I waited to see if anyone would write a book like this and make the idea more than theoretical. When I didn't see it, I decided to finally write one.

What you are holding in your hands is another first: a book composed entirely of fifty chapters of fifty words each, revealing an extended narrative. It is an Afrosurreal story of two people who find themselves alone in a city, exploring the differences between being alone and being lonely.

I hope that you enjoy this book and that other writers will consider writing in this form in the future.

— Ran Walker

Love is the selfishness of two people.

— ANTOINE DE LA SALE

THE NEW JIM CROW

1

Of all the bookstores, he chose Le Book—
just off Peppermint and Cane—for his
Saturday afternoons. Nothing marked it as special: not the shelves, nor the street. Yet it held
her presence, her quiet preference. And so, he
returned, week by week, to the pages she might
have touched.

Many bookstores were closer to their building, but she favored this one—for reasons he never knew.

He kept returning to Le Book, again and again, pretending chance brought him there.

He liked the illusion: their meetings weren't planned, but guided by fate, brushing past her as if by accident.

Though he lingered more than chance allowed, he never considered it stalking. No malice stirred in his chest—only longing, quiet and unspoken. Nevertheless, he saw now how meaning lived in the eyes of others. Intent was personal. Perception, not. Even longing, it seemed, could wear the mask of trespass.

4

They lived in the same newly-constructed building, twenty-second floor, doors apart, yet their words never stretched beyond "hello," or the hollow pleasantries of passing. What made the silence stranger—almost cruel—was that no one else lived on that floor. Just them. Two spirits orbiting one another in unfinished sentences.

5

———

e didn't know who else lived above or below them. Maybe they'd been tricked, too, into buying dreams in an empty building.

Sometimes he wondered if she craved quiet like he did—or if she felt marooned, left behind with just one neighbor who appeared too often to be coincidence.

Their interactions were brief but kind, as warm as moments between strangers could be. Her voice had become a melody he looked forward to, soft and familiar, but each time he tried to speak beyond hello, butterflies overtook him, keeping her warmth from unfolding into anything more than possibility.

*L*e Book was a strange name for a bookstore. The "Le" begged for French, but "Book" refused to play along. *Le Livre* made more sense. *Les Livres*, even better. He liked its oddness. Like the city. Like her. It felt mismatched on purpose—imperfect, and somehow more beautiful that way.

He wondered how she'd drifted into the city—what winds carried her to the bookstore, the building, this quiet life beside his. Had fate placed her gently near him, or had she chosen it all? One day, he hoped she'd tell him. Until then, he rewrote her story in dreams.

While journaling over chai, he sensed her watching from across the café. He looked up, expecting her to glance away—but she didn't. Her gaze held his, steady and soft. There was no judgment, only recognition. In that moment, it felt like she truly saw him—for the first time.

10

———————

He had spent too many Saturdays there to turn back—afternoons in the bookstore, silent waves exchanged. Now, standing, the ground beneath him seemed to vanish. The distance between them closed, and his heart quickened. There was no turning away. The moment had arrived, and he could now embrace it.

11

———

"Hi," he said, his voice soft, yet deep. He had practiced this moment more times than he would have ever cared to admit.

"Hi," she responded.

"I believe we're neighbors."

She nodded, then began to chuckle. "I was beginning to wonder if you were ever going to speak to me."

12

*H*is words began softly, hesitant as if he sought perfection in the moment, unaware that she, too, was determined to let it unfold. After a quiet lunch of deli sandwiches near Le Book, the last remnants of distance slipped away. The ice melted, and something unspoken bloomed between them.

13

After four hours, the silence between them had unraveled, replaced by laughter and ease. They moved through each moment like a shared melody, discovering rhythms in one another's words. It was inevitable now—an unspoken truth. The night would be theirs. They would fall asleep, their words suspended in time.

14

The following afternoon, they walked the length of the promenade, the city fading behind them as they gazed at the river's quiet majesty below. He hesitated, unsure whether to reach for her hand, fearing rejection, but she, with a soft smile, intertwined her fingers with his, and he exhaled softly.

"I've always felt alone," she said, leaning against the railing, her gaze fixed on the bridge in the distance.

"Me, too."

"This is different," she whispered, gesturing between them. "This is new."

"That's what makes it right," he replied.

The conversation now complete, their lips met, sealing this unspoken truth.

16

He had dreamt of her kisses for months now, and they surpassed every expectation. Her lips were softer than he had imagined. She nibbled his lower lip gently, a mischievous glint in her eyes. In that moment, he became the river, flowing beneath the bridge that now held them both.

17

They danced alone in the darkness of a room that could have belonged to either. In that moment, it did not matter. Come what may, the space was theirs, defined only by their presence. Together, they wove a silent story, each step setting the stage for something that defied expectation.

———

They allowed intimacy to unfold like a delicate, inebriating dessert.

His lips traced the curve of her neck, his breath warm against her skin. She met him with quiet hunger, her body responding to the rhythm between them. Each touch was a question, each kiss an answer, no practice needed.

19

———

The bed undulated beneath them, as the Earth itself had trembled upon its own creation, their clothes discarded in the wake of a journey toward the paradise they'd conjured from their deepest dreams.

"But we just met..." neither spoke, knowing that some things stir from the soul, needing no explanation.

20

Their conversations flowed between intense, fleeting moments of passion and simple meals, little more than sustenance. When they finally drifted off to sleep in each other's arms, they knew there was more to this than infatuation, yet they felt no need to define it, letting the connection speak for itself.

When they finally emerged from their cocoon, something felt different. As they stood together, naked, at the bedroom window, it became clear: they were alone—not just in the apartment or on their floor, but in the city itself, now eerily silent, as if civilization had vanished without a trace.

On that first day, they didn't dwell on the mystery of their solitude. Instead, they became virtuosos of each other's longing, their bodies playing a duet, each touch a note, each kiss a chord. In the silence, they crafted a melody all their own, resonating with a harmony beyond words.

The following day, something in the silence of the city seemed to *scream* for their attention.

Neither owned a television, and the phone numbers they dialed rang endlessly.

"It's like being trapped in an empty amusement park,"she said.

He nodded, swallowing hard.

"They call it liminal space," she added.

A bodega on the corner sat eerily still, its door slightly ajar, beckoning them inside.

"Hello?" she called out into the silence.

He scanned the aisles, the hum of refrigeration the only sound breaking the stillness.

At the risk of stating the obvious, he sighed and replied, "We are alone."

Standing in the center of Chocolate Avenue, they shouted in unison then in cacophonic syncopation, their voices echoing in the empty streets.

"Could an entire city really vanish?" he wondered.

"I suppose so. Remember Roanoke?"

They shouted once more, but the empty silence swallowed their words, and no one answered.

They returned to the bodega, gathering food and water.

"Do you think everyone evacuated and we missed the notice?" he asked.

"I didn't hear anything," she replied, realizing the absurdity of her words. They weren't exactly quiet lovers.

"Should we leave or stay?"

She shrugged, uncertainty lingering in the air.

They decided to wait another day, watching the streets for any sign of life. They knew they should be concerned, yet strangely, they weren't. Instead, they embraced the silence, using the absence of others as an invitation to indulge in wild unrestrained, erotic fantasies, played out in public, without shame.

28

They drifted in and out of random stores, naked, once collapsing in the middle of Chocolate Avenue. Their brown skin glistened with sweat, backs marked by asphalt imprints from shifting positions. The danger of it all felt real, yet somehow distant, an illusion woven from the thrill of their freedom.

If any two other strangers were faced with the vast possibility of unending loneliness, they might have sought answers—scientific, sociological, even spiritual.

But not them.

Each had flourished in their solitude, so complete that loneliness had no meaning.

Now, they had each other, and that, in itself, was enough.

30

They agreed to stay together, no matter what. For them, it wasn't about repopulating the Earth, like some ancient myth. It was about preserving their newfound bond. For all they knew, others might still exist, just beyond the bridge—but that was a world they no longer cared to find.

31

They'd read the stories—the last two people on Earth, the familiar tropes.

But as Black people, they understood something deeper: the weight of racism no longer hung above them like Poe's pendulum.

No more class. No more creed.

Only skin, breath, time—freed from burdens once born in silence.

How might Eden have looked to Adam and Eve? Was it grander than this city—less steel, more sky? Did they feel small, like insects beneath towering leaves?

Paradise was the word they'd been given, but here, among silent streets, that word felt ill-fitting, too soft for the vast emptiness.

As days passed, neither could recall a time when they had seen others.

Was anyone else in Le Book that day?

Had they ever actually seen a neighbor?

Their memories blurred.

It no longer seemed impossible. Perhaps they had always been alone, two souls drawn together through quiet, forgotten time.

Once, half-joking, he asked if they might actually be inside a simulation, some quiet experiment, like that old *Twilight Zone* episode.

"Perhaps," she said. "But how would we ever really know?"

"You're probably right."

For a single moment, they allowed themselves to believe it, clinging to the comfort of doubt.

They'd accepted that somehow the lights would keep shining, at least for now.

Eventually, it would end—everything does. Change was certain, both blessing and curse, but how they saw it, that was theirs to decide.

Perspective, like prayer, was a quiet act of faith.

And they believed, for now.

There was plenty: food and drink, clothes and comfort, and best of all, books and art.

Though nudity was now effortless, they chose to dress. Part habit, part ritual, part quiet armor, a gesture of readiness, should the stillness shift.

The world was peaceful—for now—but peace, they understood, was never guaranteed.

"What if there are others out there?" she asked one evening on the promenade.

"It's Fermi's paradox," he said. "If they were, wouldn't we have seen them?"

"Maybe," she whispered, "we just haven't looked hard enough."

A pause.

A nod.

Though his heart resisted, he agreed.

Her hope was contagious.

38

With no trains to ride, no bicycles to borrow, they walked—miles in all directions—searching for signs of life.

Eight paths led to the edge of the island city.

Each time, the same result.

Across the bridges, possibility waited, mute and motionless.

Even hope, it seemed, made no sound.

ould others have been evacuated—or raptured away?

Sure. By now, anything felt possible.

Was it likely? Probably not.

This was their *Blue Lagoon*, a world remade for two.

Only then did they begin to grasp the weight of it—not just the solitude, but the sheer privilege of survival.

They took their hygiene seriously now: brushing their teeth six times a day, showering, exercising, embracing a vegetarian diet.

If sickness came, they knew they'd be on their own, so they stayed proactive, treating their bodies like fragile things that needed care, out of respect for their delicate, shared life.

41

It was her idea to return to Le Book, where everything had begun. The corner of Peppermint and Cane remained eerily silent. The door stood unlocked, the "open" sign still in the window, as if time had paused, waiting for them to step back into the space they once shared.

---

*E*ventually they made their way to the cafe at the back of the store. The cafe tables were clean—except for one.

On its tabletop sat a sheet of paper with handwritten blocked print.

THE ONLY WAY OUT IS THROUGH THE BACK DOOR.

"I guess that's for us," she said.

43

———

They exited Le Book onto Cane Street, and something in him felt as if they might see a bustling street, full of people, but they didn't. He wondered if she felt the same, if she missed other people, too, but he chose to focus on her fingers interlocking with his.

"I don't get it," she said. "Why would there be a note if we are the only ones here?"

No matter how he flipped it around in his head, he felt the note had definitely been intended for them. They simply failed to understand what it was supposed to mean.

45

———

*E*ventually she developed a theory about the note they had found: the words "BACK DOOR" had nothing to do with the back door of any building.

Because the note was in all caps, she now understood that "BACK DOOR" was an actual location.

Now they just had to find it.

They combed through the phone book, tracing the white and yellow pages for any mention of "Back Door."

In a city so vast, only one place appeared: an antique shop on the east side.

Whatever they sought, it seemed, would wait for them there, so they followed their only lead.

On their first walk to the east side of the city, neither had noticed a place called Back Door, but it was impossible to know every building in a city that big. The only thing they did remember was that it had taken them nearly two hours to get there.

48

After accidentally walking past the address several times before locating the storefront, they finally found the shop housed between two cavernous brownstones, a sliver of a building as opposed to a fully developed structure.

In small letters stuck to the front door like an afterthought were the words "Back Door."

49

———

There was no window on the front of the building, so she knocked, then called out to anyone inside.

Silence.

"I can kick it in," he said, stepping back.

She paused. "Wait. I have one more idea."

He watched, curious, as she stepped back slowly and reached for his hand.

They circled around to the alley behind Back Door.

Could it really have been this simple?

She reached for the knob, but he stopped her.

"Whatever happens, know that I'm with you," he said.

She smiled, then turned the handle.

Together, they stepped through, leaving the world they knew behind.

ACKNOWLEDGMENTS

Thank you to my wife and daughter, my parents, my brother and his family, my wife's family, my fellow writers, my colleagues, my students, and those who have supported me on this strange and interesting creative journey.

Also, thank you to César Aira, Ana María Shua, Stuart Ross, Grant Faulkner, Meg Pokrass, and Toby MacLennan, all of whom helped me to appreciate this form of writing.

ABOUT THE AUTHOR

Ran Walker (he/him) is the author of 40 books. His short stories, flash fiction, microfiction, and poetry have appeared in a variety of anthologies and journals. Prior to becoming a writer and educator, he worked in magazine publishing and practiced law in Mississippi.

He is the winner of the Indie Author Project's 2019 National Indie Author of the Year Award, the 2019 Black Caucus of the American Library Association Best Fiction Ebook Award, the 2018 Virginia Indie Author Project Award for Adult Fiction, and the 2021 Blind Corner Afrofuturism Microfiction Contest. Ran is an Associate Professor of English and Creative Writing at Hampton University and teaches with Writer's Digest University. He lives in Virginia with his wife and much better half, Lauren, and his amazing daughter, Zoë.

ALSO BY RAN WALKER

B-Sides and Remixes

30 Love: A Novel

Mojo's Guitar: A Novel/ (Il était une fois Morris Jones)

Afro Nerd in Love: A Novella

The Keys of My Soul: A Novel

The Race of Races: A Novel

The Illest: A Novella

Bessie, Bop, or Bach: Collected Stories

Four Floors (with Sabin Prentis)

Black Hand Side: Stories

White Pages: A Novel

She Lives in My Lap

Reverb

Work-In-Progress

Daykeeper

Most of My Heroes Don't Appear On No Stamps

Portable Black Magic: Tales of the Afro Strange

The Strange Museum: 50-Word Stories

Bees + Things + Flowers: Microfictions

The World Is Yours: Microfictions

Can I Kick It?: Sneaker Microfiction and Poetry (with Van Garrett)

The Golden Book: A 50-Year Marriage Told In 50-Word Stories

Keep It 100: 100-Word Stories

A Burst of Gray: A Novel In 100-Word Stories

The Library of Afro Curiosities: 100-Word Stories

Black Marker: A Novel in 100-Word Stories

GloKat and the Art of Timing: A Novel in 100-Word Stories

A Different Kind of Christmas Story: A Carol in 100-Word Stories

Spaceships Don't Come Equipped with Rearview Mirrors: 50-Word Stories

This Is Not a Poem/Story: 100-Word Stories

Parts of Speech: 100-Word Stories

Four Suits: A Deck of 100-Word Stories

O'ahu: Prose Poems

Apollo's Toy Box

One Hundred Ways: A Handbook for Writing 100-Word Stories

The Night Before the End of the World

Fragments of the Afroverse: 100-Word Stories

Deux

www.ingramcontent.com/pod-product-compliance
Lightning Source LLC
Chambersburg PA
CBHW040913010826
48978CB00013BB/1270